AESOP'S FABLES

The Maid and the Milk Pail

RETOLD BY MARY BERENDES • ILLUSTRATED BY NANCY HARRISON

The Child's World

Distributed by The Child's World®
1980 Lookout Drive • Mankato, MN 56003-1705
800-599-READ • www.childsworld.com

ACKNOWLEDGMENTS
The Child's World®: Mary Berendes, Publishing Director
The Design Lab: Art Direction and Design
Red Line Editorial: Editing

LIBRARY OF CONGRESS CATALOGING-IN-PUBLICATION DATA
Berendes, Mary.
  The maid and the milk pail / by Mary Berendes ; illustrated by Nancy Harrison.
    p. cm. — (Aesop's fables)
  Summary: A maiden's daydreams of what she will buy with the money she expects
to earn for a pail of milk she carries on her head earn her a valuable lesson, instead.
  ISBN 978-1-60253-526-8 (library bound : alk. paper)
 [1. Fables. 2. Folklore.] I. Harrison, Nancy, 1963- ill. II. Aesop. III. Milkmaid and
her pail. English. IV. Title. V. Series.
  PZ8.2.B46925Mai 2010
  398.2—dc22
  [E]   2010009977

Printed in the United States of America in Mankato, Minnesota.
July 2010
F11538

Don't make plans based on things that haven't happened yet.

One day a milkmaid was walking to market. She was on her way to sell some fresh milk.

The milk was in a silver pail.
The maid had learned to
carry the pail by balancing
it on her head.

As she walked, the maid
began thinking about what
she would do with the money
she would get for the milk.

"I'll buy some chickens from Farmer Brown," she said, "and they will lay eggs each morning. When those eggs hatch, I'll have even *more* chickens. I'll have more eggs, too!"

"Soon I will have enough money to buy the blue dress I've wanted," the milkmaid thought some more, "and some blue ribbon to match. Oh, I'll look so lovely!"

"In fact," the maid thought to herself, "I'll look so lovely that all the boys will want to dance with me at the fair. All the girls will be jealous. But I won't care—I'll just toss my head at them…like this!"

The milkmaid tossed back her head. With that, the pail flew off, and the milk spilled all over the road!

The milkmaid had to return home and tell her parents what had happened.

"My child," said her mother, "never count your chickens before they've hatched."

In other words, don't make plans based on things that haven't happened yet!

AESOP

Aesop was a storyteller who lived more than 2,500 years ago. He lived so long ago, there isn't much information about him. Most people believe Aesop was a slave who lived in the area around the Mediterranean Sea—probably in or near the country of Greece.

Aesop's fables are known in almost every culture in the world, in almost every language. His fables are even *part* of some languages! Some common phrases come from Aesop's fables, such as "sour grapes" and "Never count your chickens before they've hatched."

ABOUT FABLES

Fables are one of the oldest forms of stories. They are often short and funny, and have animals as the main characters. These animals act like people. Often, fables teach the reader a lesson. This is called a *moral*. A moral might teach right from wrong, or show how to act in good, kind ways. A moral might show what happens when someone makes a poor decision. Fables teach us how to live wisely.

Mary Berendes has authored dozens of books for children, including nature titles as well as books about countries and holidays. She loves to collect antique books and has some that are almost 200 years old. Mary lives in Minnesota.

Nancy Harrison was born and raised in Montreal. She has worked as an art director, creative director, and advertising executive with clients all over the world. After relocating to Philadelphia, she began working as a freelance illustrator. Nancy's work has been published in dozens of magazines and over 30 children's books. Nancy currently lives in Vermont.